WITHDRAWN
Baldwinsville
33 East Genesee Street
Baldwinsville, NY 13027-2575

APR 2 6 2008

The Last Days of Eugene Meltsner

D1115082

WITHDRAWN

APR 2 6 2005

FOCUS ON THE FAMILY PRESENTS

— ADVENTURES IN —

ODYSSEY

NEW SERIES

WITHDRAWN
Baldwinsville Public Library
Baldwinsville, NY 13027-2575

The Last Days of Eugene Meltsner

MARSHAL YOUNGER

{Based on the teleplay by Bob Vernon}

TYNDALE
KIDS

TYNDALE HOUSE PUBLISHERS, INC.
WHEATON, ILLINOIS

WITHDRAWN

Visit Tyndale's exciting Web site at www.tyndale.com

Copyright © 2000 by Focus on the Family. All rights reserved.

Cover and interior illustrations: Vaccaro Associates, Inc.

Adventures in Odyssey is a registered trademark of Focus on the Family.

Designed by Julie Chen

Edited by Linda Piepenbrink

APR 2 6 2006

Scripture quotations are taken from the *Holy Bible,* New International Version®. NIV®. Copyright © 1973, 1978, 1984 by International Bible Society. Used by permission of Zondervan Publishing House. All rights reserved.

This novel is a work of fiction. Names, characters, places, and incidents are either the product of the author's imagination or are used fictitiously. Any resemblance to actual events, locales, organizations, or persons, living or dead, is entirely coincidental and beyond the intent of either the author or publisher.

Printed in the United States of America

06   05   04   03   02   01
9   8   7   6   5   4   3   2

Contents

THE ANTS were having a nice, quiet day. But then came the rumbling. . . .

The ant family had been taking a walk around the block after a long, hard day of working on their farm. The father ant was telling his children about the harsh outside world where he had grown up. "When I was young, an ant had to keep one eye on his work and one eye on the giant humans around him," Father Ant said as they returned home. He could still remember horror stories of entire ant neighborhoods being squashed by a single tennis shoe or bicycle wheel. His son shook off a chill.

But not here. Life in a store-bought ant farm was peaceful. The ants lived in a glass box, where no person could stomp on them or eat them or fry them with a magnifying glass. It was a world of work, sleep, and a wonderfully tangled network of tunnels. Ant heaven.

Father Ant leaned back in his lounge chair (half of a sunflower seed hull) and chuckled. His kids would never know the real fear of living on the outside.

All of a sudden, Mother Ant's favorite vase (the hollow thumb from a child's porcelain doll) fell off the mantel and shattered. She ran into the living room, wondering which of her children was responsible. But none of them had done it. So who or what *was* responsible?

Rumble. . . .

The ground shook underneath them. The first thought that came to Father Ant's mind was that a human was carrying the glass-enclosed ant farm somewhere. But when he peered through the glass, the world outside was not moving. The ground shook again, this time harder. Father Ant ran to his children and covered them with his body. The walls crumbled around them. The floor below their feet began to disappear, and the ants fell into the tunnel under their home. Sand threatened to bury them.

The rumbling got worse, and soon they were able to hear it clearly—a low, distant thunder that grew louder and louder every second. Father Ant scanned the area and discovered that the entire ant farm was caving in around them.

His son struggled to his side, and they both watched as something foreign came barreling toward them. Father couldn't make out what it was, but it looked almost like . . . a water-skier?

The family huddled together, gripped in fear—the same fear Father had experienced on the outside. As they looked at the figure coming toward them, it slowly took shape. Could it be? No. There's no way. . . . How? Was it . . . a human?

Father knew that shape. It was a human all right, but a tiny version—one that was no bigger than they were! No, wait, *two* humans . . . and they were skiing on the sand! Pulled by Ant Mildred, Uncle Fred Ant, and all their children! Their relatives had harnesses around their necks and were working in teams to pull along these two human children on the sand. And it looked like one of the kids—a boy—was actually having fun! How could he enjoy destroying their homes? What kind of human was this?

It was the Dylan Taylor kind. Dylan was a 12-year-old boy who never had an adventure he didn't like. He slid back and forth along the dunes. His younger sister, Jesse, was following along behind him, her face displaying utter terror.

"Banzai!" Dylan shouted as he jumped a "wave" of sand, performing a perfect back flip and landing on his feet.

Jesse veered to her right to avoid the wake. She was trying her best to make her ski run as unadventurous as possible. She was just hoping to hang on to the reins long enough for these ants to get tired and quit.

Dylan yelled, "Hey, Jess! Is this fun or what?"

Jesse didn't dare answer him; she might get distracted and crash. But in her head she yelled, *No!*

Dylan didn't even notice his sister's fear. "I knew you'd like it! Now hang on . . . 'cause here's where it gets really good!"

Suddenly, the ants up ahead of them disappeared down a steep ravine. Jesse's eyes bulged. They were flying off a cliff!

"Ahhhhhhhh!" Jesse screamed.

The ground ended underneath them. Dylan leaned back and lifted the front of his ski board as high as it would go. The reins pulled tight and jerked him back down. A slight moment of fear, and then a rush of wind and sand hit him in the face. His eyes teared up, but he screamed with delight.

Jesse bent at the waist, closed her eyes, and prepared to crash. She hovered in midair for a split second and then was quickly pulled down.

The angle of the cliff was as steep as the side of a skyscraper. But somehow the kids didn't crash as their skis touched the ground and continued forward. Jesse's ponytail stuck straight out from the back of her head.

She opened one eye long enough to see the ants ahead of her scramble into a large hole and disappear.

Dylan and Jesse followed the ants into the hole. It led into a tunnel that twisted and turned like a water slide. Jesse's body was jerked back and forth until she couldn't take it anymore. She steered over to Dylan and leaped, climbing onto his back.

"Hey!" Dylan shouted.

Jesse kicked off her ski board and wrapped her legs around his waist.

"Get off!"

The force of their speed sent them high up into a steep turn.

"Jess! I can't see!" Jesse's hands covered her brother's eyes. Not that he could have seen anything anyway in the pitch-dark tunnel.

But then there was a light.

"We're leaving the tunnel!" Jesse yelled, choosing to give Dylan an update on the situation rather than move her arms and let him see for himself.

Out of her one opened eye, Jesse could see something she didn't want to see. Still at full speed, they were heading straight for a fence! The ants seemed unconcerned as they veered closer and closer to the fence.

Holding the reins with one hand, Dylan used his other hand to try to pry Jesse's hands off his eyes. But her hands were stuck there like suction cups.

"Look out!" Jesse screamed.

"My eyes!" Dylan shouted.

The ants barreled toward the fence and swerved to the right just inches from crashing into it. But the skiers couldn't make the turn.

Smash! They tore into the fence. Dylan let go of the reins, and he and Jesse were launched high into the air. Like platform divers, their bodies twisted and turned together. Jesse still hung tightly to Dylan's waist.

"Woooooooooooooah!"

Jesse closed her eyes. They both prepared for a jarring impact.

Boing!

Boing? How could there be a "boing" at the end of this fall? Why hadn't they felt the impact of the ground? Jesse opened her eyes and investigated. Dylan pulled Jesse's arm off his face and looked around.

They were caught in a giant net. It stretched from a tall green windmill over to a large green barn, and they were in the middle of the two. What luck!

"Jesse, are you OK?"

Her lips trembling, she managed to say, "Yeah, I think so. That whole thing was just so—"

"Awesome!" Dylan finished her sentence, but not in the way she'd intended. "Hey, let's get out of this net and try it again!"

The net had a strange texture to it. It was sticky. Jesse

peeled part of it off her leg, but then it stuck to her hands like chewing gum. Dylan struggled with it as well.

"What is this stuff?" he said.

Dylan thrashed around so much that he became more caught in the net than he'd been at first. He could barely move his arms. He thrust his hand forward, ripping the net but wrapping himself in it even more. Jesse realized she was getting more and more stuck and looked around for help. They were on an ant farm—perhaps there was a pitchfork or something lying around that they could use to free themselves. But as she surveyed the area, she realized something. She had seen this type of net before.

"Dylan . . . this isn't a net. This is a spider web!" Jesse's discovery gave her a new reason to get out of there quickly. No telling when the owner of this web would be back to check what had come home for dinner. She threw her arms around, getting herself more entangled.

"This ant farm didn't come with spiders," Dylan said, laughing off the possibility.

"It's not funny, Dylan! Maybe a spider got inside somehow. We could both be—" She stopped when she saw Dylan's face. He had suddenly grown concerned. He was looking over her shoulder at something. She slowly turned her head. A shadow fell over both of them. A dark, black, round shape appeared. It moved closer and closer.

"Oh, no!"

With the shadowy creature inching nearer, Dylan and Jesse flailed around to get free, but by this time they had gotten so entangled that they could barely move. They were powerless against the oncoming beast.

"Can't . . . get free!"

"It's getting closer!"

The black object moved slowly, almost teasing them. The shadows were fading, and Dylan was able to make out more detail—a head, a face, a nose, a pair of glasses. . . .

Glasses?!

"Aha!" the creature shouted.

It was Eugene Meltsner, a stern look on his face. He flipped a giant switch, and the web faded around them. They were back in their virtual reality chairs. Their imaginary adventure had come to an abrupt halt.

Dylan and Jesse swiveled their chairs around to face Eugene. He was standing at the edge of the room, pushing switches and turning knobs.

"Eugene!" said Jesse, breathing a sigh of relief.

"Oh, Eugene! For a second there we thought we were in big trouble!"

Eugene stepped closer, suddenly as threatening to them as the spider would have been. "Let me assure you both . . . you *are* in big trouble!"

IT HAS BEEN said that curiosity killed the cat. Fortunately the same isn't true of humans, or Dylan Taylor would have been dead ten times over by now. If there was a closed door anywhere near him, he had to see what was behind it. The bad thing about that was that a lot of the time, there was trouble behind that door.

Dylan had never shied away from adventure. Much of the time he dragged his sister, Jesse, along for the ride. She was always telling Dylan, "Don't do that!" but of course this made Dylan want to do it all the more.

For most kids, a curious mind might not be a very big deal. But Dylan lived in Odyssey, where there were tons of things to be curious about, especially at a place called Whit's End. To the uncurious mind, Whit's End was simply an ice-cream shop. But people who had checked it out knew that it was much more. On every floor, in every room, and around every corner, there was always something new to discover at Whit's End. For Dylan, it was a place of learning and fun.

The manager of Whit's End was John Avery Whittaker, or, as most adults called him, "Whit." He was a businessman, a writer, an inventor, and quite possibly the wisest man in Odyssey. He always had something to teach, and he had the most creative ways of teaching it.

The newest of Whit's inventions—the Micro-Simulator—let humans see miniature worlds, like bugs and microorganisms. . . .

And ants. When Dylan first laid eyes on the Micro-Simulator, his mind flew to all the possibilities. He ran home and got his ant farm. He took it back to Whit's End and placed it in the Micro-Simulator. Following a few printed instructions, he put some of the dirt and a couple of ants on a slide and placed it under the Micro-Scanner. A bright beam scanned the slide and analyzed it, creating a virtual version of the entire ant farm. Then he and Jesse got into their seats and prepared to experience the world of ants for a while. Jesse was a willing participant until Dylan suggested they harness ants and go sandskiing.

That was the reason Eugene was now pushing them out of the Micro-Simulator and into the lab, his eyes still bulging out of his head. He wanted the Micro-Simulator to be used for serious projects, not for silly pursuits like sandskiing. Dylan thought Eugene sometimes took life a little too seriously.

Dylan and Jesse sat next to a table in the lab, a large metal room with test tubes, burners, and the insides of machines scattered around. Dylan stuck out his bottom lip and blew out to make his uncombed brown hair fly upward. Jesse gnawed on her fingernails.

Bernard Walton, the local janitor and a regular sight at Whit's End, was on the other side of the room washing the windows. He didn't really want to be a part of this scene, but he happened to be in the wrong place at the wrong time.

Connie Kendall, a teenage employee at Whit's End, stood behind Jesse and Dylan, waiting for a verdict from Eugene. She had her hands on their shoulders and was offering comfort during the wait. Eugene paced back and forth in front of them like a trial lawyer.

Both Dylan and Jesse had empty feelings in their stomachs, like children who had just been caught spray-painting the neighbor's garage.

Connie came to their defense. "Eugene, they didn't hurt anything. What's the big deal?"

Eugene stopped pacing and turned to face her. "The

'big deal,' Miss Kendall, only happens to be endanger-ing the advancement of medical science!" Eugene fully anticipated that the Micro-Simulator would soon be used by surgeons to see inside the human body in order to perform surgery.

"I'd better take cover," Bernard mumbled to himself. He could sense that an argument was coming.

"But Eugene, you've never not allowed the kids ac-cess to inventions like the Imagination Station before," Connie pleaded.

"That is not true, and it's also a double negative," Eugene said. Even in the heat of a debate, he simply could not allow this misuse of the English language to pass.

"What?!"

" 'Never not.' The correct vernacular would be '*al-ways* allowed access to the Imagination Station.' Which is not true."

"You're confusing me," Connie said. He was often doing that.

"That makes two of us," Bernard mumbled again.

"I'm simply trying to encourage you to use proper English. Especially when impressionable youth are present."

"Oh, brother! Would you just stick to the subject?" Connie said.

"The point," Eugene continued, obeying her command, "is that it has always been a requirement to obtain permission before using the—"

"Well, me and Jesse *did* ask Connie," Dylan interrupted.

"Jesse and *I*," Eugene said. He looked at Connie. "Do you see? This is exactly what I had feared."

"Eugene! Dylan's trying to tell you that I gave them permission."

Eugene chuckled at her like a father amused by his five-year-old. "That may be so, but the obvious intent of the rule is that a well-qualified, highly responsible person be on hand to ensure that nothing goes wrong. The operative words here being *qualified* and *responsible*."

"I'm not *qualified?*" Connie said, hands on her hips.

"Oh boy, here we go," said Bernard, trying to clean the windows as fast as he could to get out of the line of fire. This is the way it usually went with Connie and Eugene. Their arguments would start, and then Eugene would say something that would make Connie feel stupid or inferior. Connie would take it personally, and when that happened, it was all-out war.

"I'll have you know, Eugene," Connie continued, "that Whit showed Dylan and me how to set the whole thing up."

"Sandskiing through an ant farm was not the purpose for which Mr. Whittaker intended the Micro-

Simulator to be used. The new microscopic technology we've been developing could quite possibly usher in a new age in medical research."

Connie had stopped listening. She was still stewing about what Eugene had said earlier. She turned to Dylan and Jesse. "He said I was irresponsible!"

Eugene continued his speech. "The potential significance of this breakthrough should not be jeopardized simply for the sake of . . . juvenile entertainment!" Eugene held up the ant farm as if he were going to shatter it on the table.

Connie was fuming. "So now I'm juvenile on top of being unqualified and irresponsible?"

"I didn't say you were juvenile . . . exactly," Eugene said.

Bernard noticed the ant farm and suddenly became interested in the conversation. "Say . . . is that one of those ant farms?" Bernard walked up and snatched it from Eugene's hand. "Why, I haven't seen one of these in years!"

Eugene and Connie paid no attention. Connie was too busy defending herself, and Eugene was too busy trying to defend the grand purposes of the Micro-Simulator.

"Now this brings back memories!" Bernard said, admiring the ant farm. "I can't recall. Do they include the ants with the farm?"

Dylan replied, "No, you have to find your own ants."

Bernard looked through the glass at the ants. "I had an ant farm just like this when I was a kid. In fact, I bet it was the very first pane of glass I ever washed. Where did you get it?"

"I got it for my birthday," Dylan said.

"You did not," Jesse corrected. "Mom and Dad gave that to *me* last Christmas."

"You got a doll last Christmas!"

"*And* an ant farm!"

That's when it all blew up. Dylan and Jesse went back and forth about who actually owned the ant farm. Connie and Eugene went back and forth about Eugene calling Connie irresponsible and unqualified. And Bernard began taking slow, short steps backward, casually moving away from the whole thing.

"If I've said something to offend you, Miss Kendall, then I am truly sorry," Eugene said.

"*If*? You know very well what you said!"

"Dylan, you almost got us both killed in that ant farm!"

"I did not! It's imaginary! We were never in any real danger."

"Excuse me, everyone, but I must get back to work!"

"You're not getting off that easy, Eugene!"

"I didn't ask you to tag along, Jesse!"

"Fine! Then I'm taking my ant farm back!"

"*Your* ant farm?!"

"Don't you ignore me, Eugene Meltsner!"

"Enough!!!" Eugene screamed. Suddenly, the room was still and silent. No one had ever heard Eugene yell like that, including Eugene himself. He was not one to show his emotions, and this was quite embarrassing for him. He cleared his throat and tried to regain some dignity. "My apologies. I didn't mean to yell." But he was not sorry about why he had yelled. "Mr. Whittaker and I have a deadline tomorrow that is fast approaching, and I cannot allow any more distractions. Now if everyone would please leave. . . . I'm sorry."

"I'm sorry too, Eugene." Eugene turned on his heels and saw Mr. Whittaker behind him. Eugene wondered how long he had been standing there.

Long enough. Whit shook his head in disappointment and stepped toward them.

"Mr. Whittaker. I—"

"I'm sorry to see you all treating each other so poorly. Dylan and Jesse, you know better than to argue and fight." Jesse and Dylan looked at the ground. They rarely felt worse than when they'd disappointed Mr. Whittaker.

Fortunately for them, most of Whit's anger was directed somewhere else. He turned and faced Connie and Eugene. "As for you two . . . you ought to be ashamed of yourselves! Setting such a bad example in front of the kids!"

"We're sorry, Whit," Connie said. She, too, hated disappointing Whit.

"I suppose I allowed the stress of tomorrow's deadline to influence me," Eugene said—his attempt at an apology.

"And that's another thing," Whit continued. "Since when did projects become more important than people around here? How we treat those around us matters much more than any accomplishment or deadline. That's why Whit's End has always been about people! Of course we don't mind sharing our discoveries with the scientific community, just as long as we don't lose sight of our original purpose—to serve the children of Odyssey." Whit moved toward Dylan and Jesse and placed his hands on their shoulders. "Right, kids?"

"Uh, right," they answered at the same time.

Dylan breathed a sigh of relief. He felt much more comfortable now. Mr. Whittaker had obviously forgiven them for arguing. He didn't even seem upset that they'd used his invention as a ski run. Mr. Whittaker always had a way of reminding them what was important and what was not so important. Loving God and each other was important. Winning an argument usually wasn't. Pretty simple stuff, but it was easy to forget sometimes.

"Your new invention is really cool, Mr. Whittaker," Dylan said.

Mr. Whittaker smiled. "So you enjoyed your trial run on the Micro-Simulator?"

"Yeah! It was really neat to be as small as the ants," Jesse said.

"Well, Eugene, why don't you show them what it is really designed for?"

Eugene swallowed a lump in his throat and then grabbed his personal calendar like it was a life preserver. "Uh . . . certainly. Perhaps the first of next month?"

"I was thinking that you would show them right now."

That was exactly what Eugene was afraid of. Eugene pointed to his calendar. "Mr. Whittaker, might I remind you of the extenuating circumstances we are currently facing. In less than 24 hours a panel of the nation's most prominent doctors and research scientists will be arriving here, at Whit's End, for a complete and comprehensive demonstration of the Micro-Simulator."

"I am well aware of that."

"Mr. Whittaker, if we are to put on a flawless demonstration, then we cannot afford to waste another precious second—"

"What we cannot afford, Eugene, is to continue taking each other for granted," said Whit. "Let's both just look at this as the perfect occasion to practice what we preach!"

Eugene slowly put away his calendar. He knew that Mr. Whittaker was wise. He respected everything the man said. But at this moment he thought that perhaps Mr. Whittaker had read too much into the situation. Eugene assured himself that he certainly had not taken anyone for granted. He was simply thinking about the immediate future and accomplishing something very important. Medical science history was about to be made. Taking kids on pleasure tours could wait. But he was an employee of Whit's End, and of course he would abide by his employer's wishes. *Really, though,* Eugene thought, *I've done nothing wrong.*

MR. WHITTAKER'S inventions were probably the biggest reason why Whit's End was the most popular kids' place in town. His most famous invention was called the Imagination Station. This was a machine that allowed people to experience moments in history with their imagination. Whit had programmed dozens of adventures, from the Garden of Eden to man's first walk on the moon. The person using the Imagination Station actually became a character in the adventure. It was fun, exciting, and very educational. Experiencing history for themselves was something the kids of Odyssey really looked forward to.

In the same way, Mr. Whittaker's new invention, the

Micro-Simulator, allowed people to learn through experience. Dylan had used it for entertainment, but the real purpose of the machine was to explore the wonders of the human body.

Jesse and Dylan were practically bouncing out of their shoes. They were so excited to get inside the Micro-Simulator and see the inner workings of the human body. Eugene led the way into the Bible room, followed by Connie and the kids. There, next to the much smaller Imagination Station, sat the Micro-Simulator. It looked like a combination spaceship/submarine with lots of windows, lights, and propellers. The Micro-Simulator didn't actually go anywhere, so Dylan figured the propellers were only there for effect.

The inside was like the cockpit of an airplane, though larger. Monitors and buttons were everywhere. There were four chairs for passengers, plus chairs for the pilot and copilot. Two airplane-style steering wheels jutted out from a dashboard in front. And a huge windshield bent all the way around the pilots and passengers. It was like being in one of those movie theaters where the screen is so big you have to turn around to see the whole picture. Whit had told Dylan that there were two ways to use the Micro-Simulator. One was to wear a special helmet that covered your eyes and ears so that you were actually surrounded by the sights and sounds of the adventure. That's how Dylan and Jesse had experienced the ant farm. The second way to use it was to watch the wide screens. The second way allowed more people to watch at the same time.

The windshield was dark as Dylan and Jesse took their seats, but it soon would display the fascinating adventure Mr. Whittaker had cooked up for them. They could hardly wait.

Jesse felt much better about this adventure than she had about Dylan's ant farm idea. Whit had taught Dylan the basics of running the machine, and he had been a quick learner. And the adventure had been, as it turned out, harmless. But still, she felt much safer with Eugene at the controls.

Just to be sure, she asked him about it. "This works like the Imagination Station, right, Eugene?"

"It is, in fact, based on the very same technology. But whereas the Imagination Station creates virtual realms from one's own imagination, the Micro-Simulator is much more reality-based."

Jesse nodded but didn't understand. People nodded a lot around Eugene.

Once everyone was seated, Eugene was ready to make his presentation. He turned up the lights and faced them. "I've taken a sample of my own blood and placed it on this glass slide." He held up a small glass rectangle. Jesse silently hoped she wouldn't be asked to donate blood to this experiment as well. "I simply place the sample under the onboard Micro-Scanner, where it will be fully analyzed." He turned and carefully placed the slide into a heavy-duty microscope in the middle of the dashboard. Dylan leaned forward in his seat to watch a bright laser beam shoot out and scan the slide. The machine was building a DNA replication of Eugene's bloodstream based on the blood on the slide. That would enable them to take a simulated journey through Eugene's body.

Eugene made sure everything was working, then went to his pilot's chair. With ease and grace, he started pressing buttons one after another as if he did not have to think about it. "Within that tiny drop of blood is all the genetic data the simulator needs to create a completely accurate virtual facsimile," he said.

Dylan was getting impatient. "So how long is this gonna take?"

Eugene stopped pressing buttons for a moment, checked a monitor, and, with great flair, flicked a switch marked "Start." The world beyond the windshield lit up like the beginning of a movie.

"Why, the simulation has already begun!"

There was a bright flash of light, followed by darkness. The windshield screen went out of focus for a second and then became clear. It showed a dark red tunnel with red balloons floating along inside it. Connie guessed these were the red blood cells. The sides of the tunnel were throbbing in rhythm.

"Welcome to the wonders of the human bloodstream!" Eugene said.

"Whoa!" said Dylan.

"Eugene, this is fantastic!" Connie said.

Jesse admitted it was interesting but secretly thought it was also kind of disgusting. The blood vessels weren't smooth and round as she'd thought they would be; they were pitted and marked with what looked like specks of dust.

There were two monitors hanging from the ceiling in front of the passengers. One was showing the outside of the Micro-Simulator craft as it traveled through the inside of the blood vessel. The propellers were turning, and the headlight on the front was shining forward, showing that they were heading toward a larger tunnel. The second monitor was showing a picture of the human body with all of its blood vessels featured. In the right arm, there was a white light moving slowly toward the shoulder. Jesse guessed the white light was them. They were in Eugene's right arm, heading toward his shoulder.

Eugene steered the wheel back and forth carefully, dodging oncoming white blood cells. "Mr. Whittaker and I originally designed the technology as a way of teaching children the wonders of God's creation, but the program turned out so well that we soon realized it held great promise for the medical field as well. Imagine a replication of the human body that is so exact it renders exploratory surgery obsolete!"

A buzzer went off on the control panel to Eugene's right, and it caught his attention. He swiveled on his chair to read a monitor, keeping one eye on where he was going.

"Doctors," he continued, his head bobbing back and forth from monitor to windshield, "will be able to examine their patients from the inside without . . ." Suddenly he stopped and stared at the monitor. The others didn't notice because they weren't listening to him anyway; they were more fascinated by the larger-than-life trip through Eugene's bloodstream. As Eugene stared at the monitor, he stopped watching where he was going. His hands fell limply off the steering wheel.

Connie was still in awe. "Whit and Eugene have really outdone themselves this time."

Dylan was bouncing on his seat. "This is so—"

Splat! A white blood cell hit the window, splashing some kind of liquid all over the windshield.

"Gross," Jesse said, finishing Dylan's sentence. Suddenly, more and more white blood cells were hitting the sides of the machine, jarring the passengers back and forth. Eugene was taking no care to miss them!

Dylan glanced at the monitor. It showed the Micro-

Simulator making a dangerous sharp turn. He and Jesse were thrown up against the window, and Connie landed on the floor. Eugene wasn't at the wheel!

Connie looked up as she picked herself up off the floor. "Eugene? Shouldn't you be steering?" He didn't hear her. He continued to stare at the monitor, as motionless as a mannequin.

As Dylan and Jesse sat down again in their seats, Connie looked ahead through the windshield. Her jaw dropped. It looked like something was coming right at them! The monitor showed there was some kind of membrane straight ahead, and there was no way to avoid it—especially since they'd lost their captain!

The membrane grew bigger and bigger in the front windshield, getting ready to swallow them whole. Dylan clutched the side of his seat and prepared for impact.

"Eugene!" Connie yelled.

"Look out!

"We're gonna—!"

Crash!

The sub was jolted forward. The passengers flew out of their seats.

Dylan was afraid that any second now the hull was going to break and they would be drowning in Eugene's bloodstream.

The lights in the cockpit flickered crazily, burned brilliantly for a second, and then died. The monitors cut out, and the pulsating bloodstream disappeared from the windshield. They were staring into black.

Connie was holding onto the back of Eugene's chair to steady herself. She shook her head to clear it, then checked on Dylan and Jesse. They were OK. But she went from concern to anger very quickly as she regained her balance and turned toward Eugene. He was still sitting in his chair and staring at the monitor, although it was now just a blank screen. He didn't even realize they had crashed.

"Eugene! What are you doing? Are you trying to kill us?!" She whipped his chair around so he was facing her. She was about to yell at him to his face when she noticed that he was as white as a ghost. His mouth was wide open. He stared ahead vacantly, as if she weren't even there.

"Eugene, are you all right?" Connie asked. He was still staring into space. Then after a moment, he blinked and finally focused on her.

As if nothing had happened, he stood up quickly and switched off the power. The remaining working lights went off. "Of course! I, uh . . . I just need to be . . ." His voice trailed off into nothing. He walked out the door without another word.

"What was that all about?" Connie asked. Dylan and Jesse shrugged their shoulders.

THE STRANGEST thing about Eugene's behavior was that he had missed out on an opportunity to show off. Usually when he presented a new invention he'd go on and on about it. He would fill in every detail, whether his audience cared about the details or not. He would never miss out on a chance to parade his own knowledge and talents. But in this case, he'd made the presentation, barely begun the journey, and simply quit. Why hadn't he explained what everything was? Why hadn't he blathered on about which artery was what and why the blood cells were traveling the way they were?

A meeting of the minds was held at Whit's End the next morning to discuss this very subject. Dylan and

Jesse were sitting on stools at the ice-cream counter. Connie was on the other side of the counter, leaning over so they could speak quietly. Eugene and Whit were talking just a couple of rooms away in Whit's office.

"Eugene's always going off in his own world," Dylan said. "He probably got caught up in all the numbers and just forgot about driving the ship."

"He does do that," Connie said, "but never when he's trying to impress someone."

"I think he was just embarrassed that he wrecked," Jesse said. "He lost control of the sub and ran into whatever that thing was, and he was too embarrassed to admit it. So he just left."

"Yeah, I did hear he's not a very good driver," Dylan said.

"He's not a bad driver," Connie said. "I taught him."

Dylan raised his eyebrows.

"Don't say it, Dylan."

Jesse continued. "But he would be embarrassed if he couldn't even control his own invention."

"That doesn't make sense, though," Connie said. "I saw him right before we crashed. He wasn't even watching where he was going. He was staring at the monitor."

"Do you know what the monitor said?" Jesse asked.

"Whit's gonna work on figuring that out. But I think it was just a lot of numbers and stuff."

"What could be so important about a bunch of numbers that it would make him wreck?" asked Dylan.

The bell above the door rang, and Bernard Walton walked in. He was in his work clothes—overalls and a cap that was turned up at the bill. He walked especially loudly, trying to attract attention. Much to his disappointment, no one noticed. He was hoping a large group of kids would be at Whit's End to greet him because he had some exciting news to report.

"Don't mean to bother you," he said to anyone who might be listening. "Just came by to pick up some supplies I left behind."

No one heard him. He approached the counter and tried again. "And, boy, am I gonna need these supplies! Guess you probably heard I was awarded my first large industrial contract!" Still no response. Bernard rolled his eyes and cleared his throat.

"Yessiree! The new Odyssey Commerce Building. Seventeen stories of cream-colored stone, archways, awnings, and *lots* of glass windows! Pretty good, eh?"

The kids continued to whisper to each other, none of them even realizing he had come in. Bernard had had enough. He stood 12 inches from Connie's ear and bellowed, "Well, don't get excited all at once!"

"Oh, Mr. Walton," Connie said, noticing him for the first time. "Were you saying something to us?"

"No, I normally go on for hours at a time talking to myself."

"We're just trying to figure out what's wrong with Eugene," Jesse said.

"He's been acting really strange," said Dylan.

"How long have you known Eugene? Strange is normal for him," Bernard said as he picked up his cleaning supplies.

"But this is different. Ever since he took us in the Micro-Simulator he hasn't been himself."

"I suppose stress can do that to a person. He does have that important demonstration coming up this afternoon."

"But that's just it," Connie said. "If he was worried about the demonstration, he'd be in the lab. He hasn't gone in there all morning!"

"Hmmm," Bernard said, scratching his chin with his squeegee. "Even considering it's Eugene, that *is* strange. Where is he now?"

"In Whit's office. Eugene wanted to talk to him in private."

"Well," Bernard said, heading for the door, "I wish I could stick around and help you solve the enigma we call Eugene, but I don't want to be late for my first day of work at the brand new . . . Odyssey Commerce Building." He made sure he emphasized that last part. He still wanted to impress them with his new job, but no one seemed to care. "I give up," Bernard said under his breath.

"Bye, Mr. Walton," said Jesse.

The door to Whit's office opened and out stepped Eugene. Dylan was still talking about him when Connie noticed. "Shhh! Here he comes."

Eugene's color had not improved much, and his expression was one of a person who had either been fired or given a teaspoon of castor oil.

Connie tried to act normally. "Eugene, how are you doing? We were just having some hot chocolate. You want some?"

Eugene stopped in his tracks and took a long, thoughtful breath. He stepped toward Connie and looked at her. Connie noticed that his eyes were a bit red and watery. He pursed his lips to keep from crying, and he embraced her.

"Miss Kendall," he said, practically hugging the stuffing out of her. Connie's eyes bugged out.

"Eugene?" She looked over Eugene's shoulder at Whit, searching for some answer as to why Eugene, a person usually so completely lacking in emotion, was now choking up at the mere sight of her. Whit only bowed his head.

Eugene finally pulled away. "You have been a good friend, confidant, and coworker. Thank you," he said. Connie waited for the punch line but got none.

"Eugene . . . I think you finally did it. You stuffed too much information into your head and now all the common sense is spilling out of your ears."

Eugene chuckled. "That sense of humor. Priceless."

Connie watched him carefully as he walked around the counter and reached under a back shelf.

"Dylan, Jesse, I'm glad you're here as well." He tilted his head and gave the kids a thoughtful gaze. "I just wanted to ask you all to forgive me for the way I've treated you."

Eugene rarely admitted that he was wrong about anything. Dylan and Jesse exchanged looks.

Eugene continued, pulling something out from behind the counter. "I also want to give you a small token of that remorse." He placed three presents on the counter, one for each of them.

"Presents?" Jesse said, dumbfounded.

"Wow, Eugene," Dylan said, smiling. "I don't know what happened to you, but I kinda like it!" He smiled and began tearing into his package.

Connie had already opened hers. "Eugene! This is that new bowling ball I've had my eye on!"

"Wow!" Dylan shouted. "A new laptop computer!"

"Actually, it's slightly used," Eugene said.

Jesse's package was the strangest. "Isn't this your ukulele?" Eugene had played his ukulele for them before. Perhaps he wanted someone else to pass on the misery?

"Eugene," Connie said, "what's going on? You can't give these away. These are some of your most prized possessions!"

"Material objects are unimportant, Miss Kendall. It's people who matter."

"Since when? I mean . . . when did you decide this?"

"I've . . . just been doing a lot of critical and analytical thinking. And a bit of soul searching. In Psalm 90:12 it says, 'Teach us to number our days aright, that we may gain a heart of wisdom.'"

Eugene walked to the coat tree to get his jacket. The others joined him there as he put his jacket on. He put one arm around Connie and the other around Dylan and Jesse. He pulled them in close, like a father with his kids. "I realize now that I've wasted too much time pursuing the insignificant." He let them go and headed toward the door. With a swift, dramatic turn, he addressed them again. "Mr. Whittaker was right. I've been taking you all for granted. . . . Please don't make the same mistake." He opened the door, started to step out, and then turned around, addressing them now for the last time. "Good-bye."

He left. Connie thought she saw him stop and smell a flower outside before the door closed behind him.

"Uh . . . see you later?" Dylan said awkwardly.

"No you won't," Whit said, his head still bowed low. "Eugene just quit."

the last days of eugene meltsner

five

The Heist

GEORGE GRUNDY sold his last Fudge Almond Ice Cream Bar at one o'clock that afternoon. There were still five kids waiting in line for their ice cream, but he had a job to do. So he slid the metal door closed on his ice-cream truck and got into the driver's seat. He put the truck into gear amid the protests and tears of five startled and confused children. He didn't care. He hated kids anyway. Besides, after today, he'd never drive that truck again. He'd be rich.

George had lived a life of crime since he was 15 years old. Well, at least he had tried to. He had never actually committed a successful robbery, that is, if a successful robbery is defined as having three parts: (1) *stealing something* (2) *of value* and (3) *not getting caught*. He had always failed in at least one of those areas. Once he slipped a gold watch in his pants pocket while in a jewelry store. But when he got home he discovered a hole in his pocket; the watch had fallen out on the floor even before he left the store. So he had failed at the *stealing* part there.

Another time he had tried to steal some televisions that were being loaded onto a truck in front of an appliance store. While the truck driver wasn't looking, George took one. When he got home, however, he discovered the TV didn't work. Apparently the TVs were being loaded onto the truck to be taken to the trash dump. So he had failed at stealing something *of value* in that case.

Then, of course, there were plenty of times when he had stolen something of value but had been caught in the act. He had many tales of getting trapped in a revolving door, accidentally leaving the getaway car in neutral and having to run down the hill to catch it, and so on. He had spent many months in jail.

But this time would be different. He'd been plotting this ever since he got out of jail two years ago. The perfect heist. He had thought of everything. He had plans A, B, C, D—all the way through P, taking in every possibility. He had gone over the steps a thousand times in his head. It would be the most brilliant bank robbery in Odyssey history.

For two years he had waited and planned. Finally, as

the last days of eugene meltsner

he sat in his getaway car (he had checked the gear shift 13 times now) across from the Odyssey Commerce Building, the moment had come. He brushed back the small amount of hair he had left with his hand, grabbed his trench coat, and opened the car door.

Also at the Odyssey Commerce Building, but for a far different reason, was Bernard Walton. He was high up on a scaffold, washing windows outside the 14th floor.

Seventeen floors of outside windows made for an incredibly large job for Bernard. But he didn't care if it took him a month to clean all of them. His passion was washing windows. It was art for him. And he was sure he had the fastest squeegee in the west.

He whistled to himself, his squeegee hand bouncing up and down like an orchestra conductor's. *Another window done in 20 seconds flat,* he thought to himself.

He pulled down a lever to lower the scaffolding and read the side of his five-gallon drum of industrial-strength window cleaner: "Caution: Flammable!" He was using this brand of cleaner for the first time. He'd decided when he got the contract to wash the windows of the Commerce Building that he was now a big-time janitor. Big-time janitors need big-time cleaners. This stuff was extra powerful.

As he continued to conduct his glass orchestra, he heard a ringing in his ears. He thought it must be some angel janitors telling him, "Well done." But then he remembered another purchase he'd made when he got the big Commerce Building contract: a cell phone. Big-time janitors have to be able to be reached by their clients at any time. Bernard reached down to his tool belt and pulled out the phone. He was pleased as punch that someone was actually using his number.

"Walton's Janitorial Service."

"Yes, Bernard, this is Whit," Mr. Whittaker said on the other end of the line.

"Oh, hello, Whit. Do you have a janitorial emergency or something?"

"Actually, no," said Whit. "It's Eugene. He did something very strange today and I thought maybe you could help me figure it out."

"I can't understand why everybody is so surprised that Eugene is doing strange things. Doesn't anyone *listen* to the things he says?"

"He quit, Bernard."

"Quit Whit's End? Well, that *is* strange."

"He mentioned something about a death in the family. I know you're related to him. Do you know what he's talking about?"

Bernard and Eugene had found out a few years earlier that they were distant cousins. Bernard had always tried to deny it, but it was true.

"Whit, you and I both know that Eugene's an orphan. He has no immediate family."

"I know."

"Plus . . . why would he quit his job over a death in the family? He could have just taken a leave of absence."

"You're right. It makes no sense."

"I've always teased him about being wound a little too tight," Bernard said. "Maybe this time he's really snapped."

At the same moment, inside the Commerce Building, two floors below Bernard's scaffold, a customer walked into the Student Credit Union.

"Yes, Mr. Meltsner, what can I do for you?"

As dazed as he had been at Whit's End, Eugene now cleared his throat and spoke with authority. "I'd like to have a check drawn up from my savings account and made out to 'The Whit's End Children's Fund.'"

"Certainly," the teller said as she began scribbling something. "And how much would you like to withdraw?"

"All of it. I'll be closing my account."

The teller's eyes widened, and the pen fell from her hand as if she had turned to stone. She looked like she was going to scream.

Eugene was surprised by her reaction. "Ma'am, I hardly think the loss of one account—"

"Ladies and gentlemen . . . ," a voice behind him cried out. Eugene whirled around and saw a man wearing a long black trench coat and a handkerchief over the lower half of his face.

"This is a robbery!" The man laughed wildly. It was a line he had practiced in front of the mirror 200 times.

A wave of panic hit the room. Scattered screams from patrons and credit union employees filled the place. Many people ducked behind desks. Eugene stood perfectly still.

Whit slipped the cover off the back of the Micro-Simulator, revealing interweaving wires and computer circuitry. Jesse backed off, afraid she might get shocked. But Connie and Dylan figured Whit knew what he was doing. He had built the invention, after all. Whit pulled out some wires and began connecting them to a nearby television. He had never allowed a television in Whit's End before, so he was obviously going to use it in a special way. Connie had no idea what that would be.

"So you say," Whit began, "that Eugene was perfectly fine before the Micro-Simulator adventure. Right?"

"Yeah," they all agreed.

"But he started acting strangely *during* it?"

"Yeah. He stopped paying attention to steering the

ship and was preoccupied with one of the computer monitors," Connie said.

"Then I'm thinking that the Micro-Simulator itself might be able to fill in the blanks. In theory, I should be able to play back the data from your adventure directly off the computer's hard drive." Whit turned the television toward them. "If my hunch is right, then the key to our little mystery might just show up here on this television screen."

They all leaned forward as the screen lit up.

The customers and employees were still frozen in position. But bank robber George had taken his place on top of a desk. His combat boots made mud tracks on the wood as he paced back and forth, clearly enjoying his moment. His wild, buggy eyes popped out from above the bandanna across his face. You could tell, even though his mouth was not visible, that he was smiling.

He began speaking in a dramatic voice that was obviously not his real one. "Welcome to a kinder, gentler age of bank robbery! As you can see, I carry no guns and have no accomplices. . . ." Somehow, this did not calm anyone's fears. "But before anyone thinks of doing something foolish, may I please draw your attention to the device I've placed in the main entry."

Like some kind of head version of "the wave," everyone's heads turned to face the door. Sitting in the doorway was a large bomb, complete with seven dynamite sticks and a digital display, all attached to a circuit board underneath it. An antenna stuck out from the top. Eugene realized the antenna meant that someone must be carrying a remote detonator.

He was right. George turned their attention back to himself. In the palm of his hand was a small black box with a red button sticking out the top. He was pressing down on the button firmly. "In my hand I hold a radio-controlled detonator. Should anything happen to me to cause my thumb to release this pressure-sensitive button . . ."

For effect, he paused and jumped down off the table, flailing his arms around as if he was about to let the button go at any moment. "Well, let's just say it won't be pretty. It's my little way of ensuring that this job goes off without a single hitch! Even if the police arrive, my little friend here can hold you all hostage until I am safely away. You see, I've thought of everything. I've had two years to plan, and I've left nothing to chance. My plan is absolutely perfect! It's utterly useless to resist! Soon the world will hail the criminal genius of this mastermind!"

George threw his arms up in the air, tossing the hand with the red button carelessly about. His audience held its collective breath.

He stood with his arms upraised, basking in his power. His plan was working perfectly!

"Uh, excuse me," the bank manager said as he carefully stepped forward. He spoke timidly, keeping a sharp eye on the red button. "I certainly don't mean to offend, but were you aware that this institution doesn't deal in cash money?"

George slowly lowered his arms. "What?"

"To be absolutely frank," the manager continued, "we don't even have a vault."

George stopped for a long moment. Visions of stealing worthless televisions popped into his head. He leaned over, in total shock, and put his head in his hands. What he didn't realize is that when he bowed down, his bandanna slipped down to his neck, revealing his face for everyone to see.

"No vault?!"

"We're just a student credit union. Sure, we take care of savings and loans, but we just cut checks and send people down to the bank on the first floor."

George slapped himself on the side of the head. "Idiot!" he said to himself. "The bank's on the first floor."

"Oh, and one other thing," said the bank manager. "Were you aware that we can all plainly see your face?"

George felt for his bandanna but instead got his bare cheek. The man was right. His stomach turned violently.

"It's Mr. Grundy, the ice-cream man!" he heard one of the bank customers say.

It was over. The perfect heist was through. He just had to get out of there before the police arrived. He couldn't go back to jail. He had to flee.

With a quick turn, he made for the door.

Wham!

He ran smack into a closed glass door. His face smashed up against it and he slid down, falling unconscious on the floor. The customers gasped as his hand fell limp and released the red button.

Connie had never seen Whit's face so filled with horror. He was looking at the monitor in disbelief.

"Dear Lord . . . no."

"Mr. Whittaker?" Jesse asked.

"This can't be."

"What?" Connie said. "What is it? Please!"

Whit stood up and braced himself on the monitor as if he was about to topple over. He took a deep breath and began. "Eugene and I programmed the Micro-Simulator to do more than simply create a virtual representation of a human body. It also scans the entire anatomy looking for anything foreign or abnormal."

Connie's stomach twisted in knots. "It found something, didn't it?"

"Yes." Whit's mouth was dry. He licked his lips and

continued. "According to the computer, Eugene has triatoma . . . a highly aggressive degenerative disease."

"A disease?"

"But . . . ," Connie said, "he's going to be OK . . . right?"

Whit shook his head. "The prognosis is terminal."

Dylan shouted, "Mr. Whittaker, what does all that mean?"

"It means . . . Eugene is dying."

EVERYONE CLOSED their eyes, sprawled out as low as they could get to the floor, and prepared for the blast.

Silence.

Eugene carefully peered around a plant and saw that the bomb was still there—but the digital display was now counting down seconds.

Eugene did not have much of a history of courage. At Whit's End, he usually let Connie kill the spiders when it was necessary to do so. But at this point he knew that many lives were at stake. Human lives. People who had families and a future, people who mattered to God. *I'm dying anyway, so what do I have to lose?* thought Eugene.

He held his breath and walked quickly toward the bomb. The people in the bank murmured, afraid to move but also afraid not to. Heads popped up like curious gophers all around, some of them mumbling, "Look at that fool!" and "He's a dead man."

But Eugene wasn't worried about what others thought. He had a bomb to disarm. He knelt down beside it and pulled a screwdriver from his vest pocket— one of several things he kept there for emergencies. The display read *29 . . . 28 . . . 27 seconds . . .*

"Don't fail me now, little screwdriver."

Eugene's hands shook violently as the screwdriver inched toward the circuit board. His glasses fogged up and the sweat from his forehead dropped like a waterfall into his eyes. He shook his head so he could see.

He touched the board with the screwdriver. It sparked—sending a gasp through the crowd—and then the display blinked off.

Stuck at 24 seconds.

Eugene breathed deeply for the first time in what seemed like hours. He stood up like a robot, carefully cradling the bomb in his hands. He turned toward the back of the credit union. "Haste definitely makes waste," he said to himself.

"Is there a back door to a stairwell?" he asked, glancing around. He felt it would be safer to retreat to a low-traffic area.

The bank manager pointed to an exit sign in the far corner of the room.

"Everyone, please remain where you are until I can move this bomb safely out of the way."

He took one step, and everyone in the room screamed and ran out the front door toward the elevators.

Eugene walked alongside the windows toward the exit.

Bernard lowered his scaffold down to the 12th floor, the one where the Student Credit Union was located. Bernard had no idea what had just taken place inside these windows. He was off in his own janitorial world, whistling and listening to polka music on his transistor radio.

He was even getting used to the strong smell of his industrial window cleaner. He squeezed the spray nozzle, which was attached by a hose to a barrel of the liquid, and squirted the window.

His radio cut out in the middle of a song, and a newscaster came on. "We interrupt the Afternoon Polka Party to bring you this breaking news. A madman with a bomb has taken over the Odyssey Commerce Building and is threatening to set it off. We'll bring you more news as this situation develops."

Bernard barely listened to the newsbreak, but one

the last days of eugene meltsner

thing caught his attention. The Odyssey Commerce Building . . .

"But *this* is the Odyssey Commerce Building." The rest of the announcement began to sink in. There was a bomber inside the very building he was cleaning!

He took one last, quick swipe with his squeegee, across thick dirt. . . .

"Eugene!!"

Bernard's eyes shot open wide as he saw Eugene inside, carrying a bomb!

He almost lost his balance on the scaffold. "He really *has* lost it!"

Bernard had to do something. He had to talk Eugene out of it. Whit wasn't around, so that left him. *Eugene's family,* he thought. *He'll listen to me.*

Bernard pounded on the window. Three times, four times, then repeatedly.

It was as if Eugene couldn't even hear him. Actually, Eugene did, but he thought it was his own heart beating.

"Eugene! Come to your senses!"

No response.

"I've got to get through to him," Bernard said to himself. He looked around and picked up the big metal barrel. He had to do it.

Crash!

The barrel flew through the window, sending shards of glass in all directions. The noise was deafening.

Eugene looked up, thinking something had exploded, and saw a huge barrel coming right at him!

He ran with the bomb as he scrambled to get out of the way, but it was too late. The barrel struck him in the back of the knees, sending him flying. The jolt flung his hands wildly for a split second—and he let go of the bomb. It went sailing into the air in a gigantic arc.

Eugene didn't even see where it went. He was flat on the ground.

Unfortunately, Bernard didn't see the bomb either. He stuck his head inside the broken window.

"Euge—"

Clunk! The bomb landed on his head, knocking him out. He fell back through the window and onto the scaffold.

The bomb bounced on the floor and rested there. There was a spark, and then the digital display resumed its countdown. *24 . . . 23 . . .*

Eugene sat up, studied his surroundings, and searched for the bomb. There it was—and the digital display was lit up.

It was counting down!

He scrambled over to it on his hands and knees. *20 . . . 19 . . .*

His screwdriver was missing. He fumbled around his vest, in each and every pocket. Nothing.

Eugene frantically crawled across the floor, his head jerking in every direction.

"It's got to be here somewhere!" he said aloud.

Meanwhile, by the front glass doors, George Grundy awoke. He shook his head and was surprised to find that all of his hostages were gone.

"Hey! Where'd everybody go?" He felt a bump on his head, then turned to see Eugene doing a crab impersonation. Eugene turned to look at him. The timer was counting down. The screwdriver was nowhere to be found. Suddenly, Eugene had a higher purpose than disarming the bomb. He had to save this man's life.

They had to get out of there!

He jumped up and ran over to George. He pulled him up off the floor, practically tearing his arm off. "Come on. We must leave these premises immediately!"

He never even saw Bernard.

Bernard was the last of the unconscious to come to. He was lying on the scaffold, looking toward the open sky. Tiny specks of glass were scattered beside him.

He rubbed his head and sat up. "Oww. . . ." It took him a moment to get his bearings. "Eugene!"

Bernard leaped to his feet and was about to dive through the broken window when he noticed Eugene wasn't there.

How long had he been knocked out?

But then something caught his attention. He heard a

whirring sound, like electronic parts. He looked down. It was the bomb!

"I gotta get out of here!"

Eugene felt a strange surge of strength. He lifted the robber into the elevator and threw him against the wall. He quickly punched the *G* button for ground floor. The doors moved more slowly than the minute hand on a watch.

George, the robber, had a weird smile on his face as he sat comfortably against the wall. "We're not gonna make it . . . ," he said in an irritating voice.

10 . . . 9 . . .

Bernard pushed the control lever on the scaffolding as hard as he could. He'd never realized before how very slow this thing was! It inched up the side of the building like a caterpillar.

"Faster! Faster!" But there was only one speed.

8 . . . 7 . . .

The elevator wasn't going much faster. Eugene was subconsciously standing heavily on the floor, as if to give the elevator a push. His glasses fogged up again. "Let's go! Let's go!"

6 . . . 5 . . .

Precious seconds had passed, and Bernard was still only one floor above the bomb. "C'mon! C'mon!" he said, gritting his teeth. Bernard mouthed a quick two-word prayer: "Help me!"

4 . . .

"Hurry!" Eugene shouted.

3 . . . 2 . . .

Eugene squeezed his eyes shut and clenched his teeth.

1 . . .

"Kablam!" yelled the robber.

"Yaaaaaaaaaa!" Eugene screamed, his arms flailing.

Silence.

More silence.

A little more silence, then laughter. Eugene turned around. The robber was cracking up.

Bernard took his fingers out of his ears and opened one eye. He was only one floor above the bomb, and he had heard nothing. Was it a dud?

"I'm OK," he said, hyperventilating. "I'm OK!" He was so relieved, he leaned back and almost lost his balance on the scaffold. He laughed at the irony that the fall would've killed him. He would laugh at just about anything at this moment.

Eugene glared at George. "You could've killed some-one!" he yelled, finding that surge of strength again. He picked up the robber by his shoulders and pinned him against the wall.

"I never meant to hurt anybody," said the robber. "It was just some firework sparklers and road flares I taped together."

"It was inexcusable," Eugene said, still holding him against the wall.

"Nobody got hurt, did they?"

"Not that I know of." Eugene let go of him. The robber sat down again.

"No one was ever in any real danger, right?"

"Well, I suppose not."

Little did they know what was happening back on the 12th floor. . . .

The bomb actually did go off. But it was only a harmless shower of sparks.

However, the harmless shower of sparks suddenly became dangerous.

Bernard's cleaning fluid barrel had burst open when it was sent flying through the window. A slow, steady stream of flammable liquid was gurgling out of the spray hose connector.

It was inching its way across the carpet toward the sparks.

Eugene slid down the wall of the elevator to sit next to the robber. He was emotionally spent. The shirt underneath his vest was drenched with sweat. His glasses were bent and fogged up.

"I'm sorry," Eugene said. "It's just that—" He chuckled in relief. "Well, for a minute there I thought my life was about to end *very* abruptly."

The silliness of the situation hit them both. All the screaming. All the panic. It was all for nothing.

"You shoulda seen your face when you screamed."

They both started to laugh.

Upstairs, a tiny spark flickered from the fireworks and landed on the carpet. The liquid seeped toward it . . . and they connected.

A burst of flame! The fire zigzagged down the narrow path of cleaning liquid toward the barrel.

Eugene and the robber were laughing so hard on the elevator floor that they were almost crying. They were now six stories beneath the raging fire on the 12th floor.

The fire raced toward the barrel. . . .

Kablam!

This one was real. A wall of windows was blown to smithereens. It was an instant inferno. The people who had evacuated the building gasped from the parking lot.

CONNIE AND WHIT sat in stunned silence. Still seated by the Micro-Simulator, they had just finished praying for Eugene, wherever he was. They also prayed for themselves, because they were losing a good friend. Whit even prayed for the community of Odyssey, for it was losing a faithful citizen.

They kept wishing they could just erase the last 48 hours and have everything be as it was before. When Whit and Eugene were creating the Micro-Simulator together, neither of them had dreamed that it would be the last project they ever did together. Whit wished he had known that. He wondered if he might have acted differently toward Eugene.

Connie was *sure* she would have. Eugene had been such a close friend. How could they have wasted so much time bickering about such silly stuff?

"If only I had known, Whit," she said.

Whit opened his Bible and read James 4:14: "Why, you do not even know what will happen tomorrow. What is your life? You are a mist that appears for a little while and then vanishes."

Connie admitted that she hardly ever treated life like that—as though it could be taken away at any moment.

"I think all of us would live a lot differently and appreciate life—and people—more if we kept that in mind," Whit said.

It wasn't a thought that helped them very much right now, though. They still had a dying friend.

There was only one thought that did help. "I'm so thankful that Eugene is a believer," Whit said. Not too much time had passed since Eugene had made a decision to trust Jesus as his Savior and Lord. It had been a long time coming, and some people thought it never would happen. But one day he had decided that the evidence was too overwhelming for him to ignore. He'd asked Christ to forgive his sin and take over his life. As a result, he'd begun studying the Bible and showing signs of spiritual growth. Now his friends were clinging to the fact that because he had given his life to Jesus, it meant that when he did die, he would spend eternity in heaven with God. This somehow made the current situation a little more bearable. Still, they were already missing their friend.

"Um, excuse me, Mr. Whittaker," Jesse said as she came in. It took a moment for Connie and Whit to realize that she had spoken. "Some doctors are here to see you."

"Doctors? Oh, that's right. The Micro-Simulator demonstration. I completely forgot. You know what, Jesse, I don't think I can do this now. Would you tell the doctors . . ." He paused.

"What is it, Whit?" Connie asked.

"Doctors. . . ."

"Do you want me to tell them to come back some other time?" Jesse asked.

"No. Right now is perfect!" Whit said. "Jesse, send them in."

A crowd of hundreds had gathered outside the Commerce Building. They all looked up helplessly at the consuming fire that had now spread to five floors. Smoke billowed, and explosions blasted out windows almost in rhythm.

Sirens could be heard surrounding the area. Fire trucks appeared, and many onlookers sighed with relief. Television crews had parked their vans and were already on the air.

"As you can see," one reporter said into a camera,

"flames from the blast have spread to various sections of the building. We think that all floors have been successfully evacuated. We now know of only two men who didn't make it out of there—the madman who caused the blast, who is reportedly the ice-cream man in town, and local citizen Eugene Belzer, who witnesses have said heroically put his own life on the line in a sacrificial effort to save the lives of others. If only he were here now to see the crowd of people who owe him a debt of gratitude."

Suddenly, in a cloud of smoke, Eugene and the robber emerged from the building. Their clothes were tattered and covered with soot. Firefighters, police officers, and television reporters rushed over.

"I didn't do it," George pleaded. "That wasn't a real bomb!" The police didn't seem to care.

"All right, Grundy, you're coming with us." They carried him off. He wondered how many years in jail he would get for this one.

Fire officials had to work their way through the wave of reporters that huddled around Eugene. Eugene raised his hand to indicate that he was OK.

The reporters persisted. "Mr. Belzner, may we have a word with you?"

Another reporter crowded in. "Mr. Seltzer, how did you get out?"

"Mr. Belcher, the entire town of Odyssey is indebted

to you for your bravery. What do you have to say to them?"

"It's Meltsner," Eugene said with difficulty. The reporters scribbled in their notebooks.

"Not only have you saved innocent lives, but you've caught the culprit who is responsible for it all. You, sir, are a true hero."

The reporter gave him a congratulatory slap on the back. It was too much for Eugene's frail and exhausted body to take. He crumpled to the ground. The other reporters scrambled to help him back up.

The reporter looked into the camera, embarrassed that he had just floored the hero of the hour. An assistant rescued him, handing over a sheet of paper. "And this just in," he said. "It seems that there is one last person still in harm's way. Firefighters have spotted a window washer trapped high on the side of the building. A rescue team is inside trying to reach him, but the flames are preventing them from getting near."

The assistant handed him another piece of paper. "Oh, and we also know that the name of the man is . . . Bernard Walton."

Eugene heard the name from within the crowd of people and pushed them aside. He grabbed the reporter's tie. "Would you please repeat that?"

"The name of the man is Bernard Walton?"

Eugene pulled himself to within inches of the reporter's face, shook him by the neck, and screamed, "Do you have access to a news chopper?"

The reporter was still on live TV and couldn't refuse the hero in front of thousands of viewers. He nodded his head, and they ran to get the helicopter.

Whit was giving the doctors a tour of the Micro-Simulator, much like Eugene had done for the kids. But Whit was not interested in how cool the doctors thought it was.

"Mr. Whittaker, this is incredible!" one of them said.

They were again heading down Eugene's blood-stream. Whit was in his pilot's chair and Dylan was behind him in a passenger's seat. Whit had asked him to be there to point out the exact time when Eugene had started acting strangely. Dylan sat quietly as the three tall men in lab coats gazed out the windshield and examined the monitors.

The doctor continued his praise. "The potential medical applications for this type of—"

"Forgive me for interrupting," said Whit, "but the real reason I gave you distinguished gentlemen this demonstration was to get your invaluable second opinion."

"About what?"

"I'd like you to look at this monitor."

All three of them ducked their heads simultaneously to get a good look.

"The blood sample we used," Whit said, "is from one of my employees. And this message came up on the monitor. I'd like you to tell me what you think."

One of the doctors nodded. "Triatoma, huh?"

Another doctor looked out through the windshield and nodded with him. "Yeah. I can see that. Right there," the doctor said, pointing at something. The third doctor seemed to agree.

"Yes, having studied entomology, I can absolutely confirm the presence of the disease."

"And it's definitely fatal?"

"Oh, yes."

Whit's eyes watered up, and his arms fell limply to his sides.

The doctor continued. "But how it found its way into this blood sample is beyond my imagination."

"What do you mean?" Whit asked.

"Triatoma is a plant disease that is carried by ants. Your sample was obviously contaminated."

Dylan slumped down in his chair. "Oops . . . ," he mumbled. He suddenly remembered that he had placed dirt from his ant farm on a slide before going on the sandskiing trip. Perhaps he had failed to wash it thoroughly.

Whit looked back at Dylan, but reproving him was secondary now. Eugene was going to live!

Connie was troubled by what she saw on the snowy TV screen. She fiddled with the dial, trying to improve the picture. It wasn't getting much better. She had to tell Whit and get down there.

Before she could stand up, Whit burst out of the Micro-Simulator door, followed by Dylan and the doctors. "Connie, it was all a big mistake! Eugene's going to be fine!"

"Oh no, he's not! Look!"

There, on the television, they saw Eugene looking out the door of a news helicopter. He was preparing to step onto the landing gear and jump down to the burning building below.

"Come on!" Whit shouted. "We've got to get to Eugene before it's too late!"

THE HELICOPTER hovered over the top floor of the building. Eugene, the news reporter, a helicopter pilot, and a cameraman were on board. The cameraman was capturing the entire event on film.

Eugene shook his head. "Can you get me any lower?" he asked.

The pilot realized that the man who was trapped on the side of the building was Eugene's friend, but he had nothing at stake. *What am I even doing up here?* he thought. "No can do. Those windows could burst out at any moment. I'm not going anywhere near 'em."

Eugene scanned the building and spotted an area

that didn't appear to be on fire. "Can you get me over there?" Eugene asked.

The pilot shook his head again. "Power lines."

Eugene was desperate. He didn't think it would do him any good to get on the roof because the fire had already spread to the top of the building. Besides, the fire department had already tried that.

Then he saw it. The scaffolding ropes. They were hung over the top of the roof and fastened securely.

"Take me over to the ropes!" Eugene shouted over the helicopter rotors. The pilot asked no questions and headed over.

They hovered over the edge of the building, and Eugene hung his legs out the helicopter door. Fire billowed out the windows, but for one split second the smoke cleared and he caught a glimpse of Bernard. He was lying on the scaffold. Eugene knew what he had to do. He would rappel down the ropes, push down the lever that lowered the scaffold, and descend slowly to the ground.

It would be tricky.

But he figured he had nothing to lose.

The reporter caught his attention before he leaped. "Before you jump out of the safety of this news helicopter down to the roof of that towering inferno—Mr. Belcher, is there anything you would like to say?"

Eugene shifted his weight, aimed for the ropes, and jumped. "It's Meltsneeeeeeerrrrrr!"

Bernard was shaken by the blast, and it took him several minutes to remember where he was. He glanced around. His clothes were covered with soot. He was still on the side of the building, but now there were hundreds of people on the ground, looking up at him. Police cars, fire trucks, and TV news vans were all pointed toward his scaffold.

The scaffold was still pretty much intact, though he had lost a couple of metal bars and the control lever looked bent. He felt the bump on his head and deduced that it had something to do with the bent control lever.

The fire was not only below him but above him as well. The windows next to him were unbroken, but he could see fire inside the building on his floor. The windows could blow any minute, and he knew it.

The fire chief, who was supervising the rescue mission from the ground, saw that Bernard had regained consciousness. He picked up his electronic megaphone. "Don't worry, Mr. Walton. . . . Things may look hopeless, but we're working on a plan." He turned to a coworker and mumbled, "Do you think he bought it?" Unfortunately, he hadn't turned off his megaphone.

"I heard that!" Bernard called back.

Panic was setting in. He had to do something. He

scrambled to his feet and grabbed the control lever. It didn't work.

He knocked on the window to see if he could break it and get inside, but it was too hot. He wondered what was worse—the fire trap inside or the concrete parking lot 13 stories below.

"Who am I kidding?" he said to himself. "I'm never gonna get out of here. It'll take a miracle. . . ."

Suddenly, out of a cloud of smoke, Eugene slid down the rope.

"Mr. Walton!"

Bernard was beside himself. "Eugene!" He smiled . . . but then he remembered how he had last seen Eugene. He had been carrying a bomb inside the bank. He was the reason this building was on fire! *Now what's worse?* Bernard thought to himself. *The fire, the concrete, or a madman coming to finish you off?*

"You stay away from me!" Bernard said, backing away as much as the tiny scaffolding would allow.

Eugene thought that maybe Bernard had been affected by his trauma. He could see no other reason why he would act this way toward him.

Eugene looked above Bernard and gasped. The scaffold ropes were on fire and about to snap!

Eugene scrambled for the control lever, but just as Bernard had found earlier, it wouldn't budge. Their only hope was to climb up the two ropes that weren't on fire.

Eugene decided he must get Bernard away from that side of the scaffold—delicately, because of Bernard's mental condition, but quickly. He held out his hand.

Bernard turned his body away. "I saw what you did, you . . . you . . ." He had no time to search for a good insult. "You building blower-upper!"

"Mr. Walton, listen to me! I need you to come to this side of the platform!"

"No! I'm staying right he—"

Snap! The rope burned through, and like a ton of bricks, the entire right side of the scaffold plunged toward the ground.

The metal railing Bernard was leaning on gave way, and Bernard fell with it.

"Bernard!"

Whit had created an invention called the Strata-Flyer specifically for emergencies like this. It was like a combination helicopter/hot air balloon, but with a number of special gadgets. It was not meant, however, to be flown as recklessly as Whit was about to fly it. "Hold on, kids," he said. Whit jammed the gear shift into drive, and the Strata-Flyer rose quickly out of its hangar. Whit made a dangerous turn, throwing Dylan, Connie, and Jesse to the floor. He would apologize later.

The side of the scaffold was in Eugene's way. He could not see if Bernard had fallen to the ground. He rappelled down the rope and sat on the wooden platform—which used to be the side of the scaffold but now was the top. The entire right side had collapsed.

He knelt down and peered over the side. There was Bernard, dangling by one hand from a rope.

"Can't . . . hold on . . . much longer!"

There were only a few inches between Bernard's hand and the end of the rope. Slowly it slid out from his grasp. He looked up as the end of the rope disappeared into his hand and out the other side. Two inches . . . one inch . . . none.

Snatch! Eugene struck like a snake and grabbed Bernard by the wrist the same moment the rope ended. Eugene was hanging upside down, his legs wrapped in the ropes above him. Bernard lifted his other hand, and Eugene was able to hold him by both wrists.

"Don't worry, Mr. Walton. I've got you!"

The Strata-Flyer sprinted toward the tallest building in town. The smoke and fire had spread to almost every floor now.

Dylan had the binoculars. "There they are!"

Whit saw them as well. He reached into the instrument panel for a telephone. "Jesse, tell Connie to stand by with that harness."

Eugene had no idea how he found the strength, but with the help of a still intact rope, he and Bernard were able to pull themselves back up to the wooden plat-form. Bernard sat down beside him. They were safe for now, but not out of danger.

Bernard tried to regain his breath. "Eugene," he said through huge gasps, "you saved my life."

Eugene did not think it was the time for gratitude, but he appreciated the gesture anyway—especially af-ter Bernard had tried to get away from him earlier. Eu-gene glanced up toward the roof of the building and was instantly horrified. The remaining scaffolding ropes had begun to catch fire. They couldn't climb back up that way!

The cell phone in Bernard's tool belt rang.

"Walton's Janitorial Service," he answered.

"Bernard, we're coming in close. Get ready to catch a safety line!" It was Whit!

They looked up, and like an angel appearing through the clouds, the Strata-Flyer emerged from the smoke. It hovered dangerously close to the building as the side hatch opened.

It was Connie. She threw a safety harness down to them, and Eugene caught it. She pulled the rope taut and stood ready to reel them in.

With one eye on the rope above them and one eye on Bernard, Eugene helped him put on the safety harness.

"It's too small! How are we both supposed to fit into this thing??"

Eugene remembered something. When he and Whit had created the Strata-Flyer together, they built the safety harness to carry one person at a time. But perhaps there was a chance. . . .

Eugene fumbled with the buckle.

They heard a snap, and the scaffold fell three inches. Bernard looked up.

"Oh, no! Look!"

The scaffold's remaining ropes were burning!

"If those ropes burn through, this whole thing is coming down!"

"The buckle is stuck!"

Snap! Another corner of the scaffold fell free. There was very little for them left to stand on.

Only two burning ropes remained.

Eugene pulled and twisted the buckle with every ounce of strength, but it wouldn't budge.

"Eugene! I don't think we're gonna make it!"

Snap! Another rope gone. Eugene held on to a metal railing.

Eugene grunted and twisted his body in ways it was not supposed to go. He had to unsnap the buckle . . . or he would die.

He would die.

Eugene stopped struggling. A peace fell over him

like a waterfall. *This is OK,* he thought. This was the inevitable outcome of his life. It was going to happen sooner or later, so there was no reason to put it off. He would die, knowing that on this last day of his life, perhaps he had done something significant. And perhaps this was a better way to go than slowly being eaten away by a disease.

Besides, he remembered, he was a Christian now. There were far greater things ahead of him. He wasn't going to a dark, scary place. He was going home—to a place where he belonged and was welcomed. A place where he would be with God for all eternity.

But he would miss his friends for a while.

He gazed at Bernard, who was now dangling safely inside the harness, and pushed him away from the burning building. "Good-bye, Bernard."

What is Eugene doing? Why isn't he trying to reach my hand? Bernard wondered.

Eugene suddenly had no fear at all.

Yes, this was best.

"What are you doing?" Bernard screamed.

Connie turned the crank, and the rope pulled Bernard from the building. He swung out under the Strata-Flyer.

"Good-bye," Eugene said again. He sat down and waited for his fate.

Bernard's phone rang.

the last days of eugene meltsner

It was dangling halfway off the platform, and Eugene absentmindedly picked it up.

"Walton's Janitorial Service, this is Eugene."

It was Whit. "Eugene, what are you doing?! Why aren't you in that harness?"

"It wouldn't fit. And I couldn't risk Mr. Walton's life for mine."

"Eugene, listen to me! Your life is just as valuable as—"

"I'm ill, Mr. Whittaker. Very, very ill. I've got—"

"Triatoma! It's an insect disease!"

"Yes, it—what?"

"It only kills bugs and plants! The slide was contaminated!" Eugene's stomach took a trip up his throat. "Hello . . . Eugene?"

"Um . . . Mr. Whittaker?"

"Yes?"

"Get me outta here!!!!"

Whit's eardrum was pierced by Eugene's scream, but that was the least of his worries at this point. Whit had the difficult task of maneuvering the Strata-Flyer as close to the building as he could, as carefully as he could, as fast as he could. But strangely enough, his hands were calm as he turned the steering wheel toward the building.

Bernard was still dangling underneath, trying to steady himself enough to be able to catch Eugene. His body swayed and turned, but once the Strata-Flyer slowed down, he came to a stop.

He clapped his hands together and urged Eugene to jump. "This is as close as we can get. Come on, Eugene! I'll catch you!"

Eugene reached forward as far as he could, but he was still a few feet away from Bernard's outstretched hands.

"I don't think I can make it!" Eugene shouted.

"Yes, you can! You can do this!"

The scaffolding shuddered. Eugene glanced quickly at the burning rope above him. It was beginning to fray.

"Now, Eugene! Now!"

It was a distance Eugene could never jump under normal circumstances. But he had done things on this day that he never would've thought he could. Perhaps it just took some faith.

He stretched out, his feet pushing on the railing underneath him, trying for as much leverage as possible.

Snap! The last rope broke. Eugene leaped across the chasm as the scaffolding plunged out from under him.

As if in slow motion, Eugene reached out in desperation, Bernard's fingertips just inches away. Eugene flung out his opposite arm, as if he were trying to fly, and stretched it out as straight as it would go.

His hand approached Bernard's, closer . . .

And missed.

"Eugene!" Bernard yelled. Eugene fell toward the earth in slow motion, his fingers still outstretched as if Bernard could somehow extend his arm out of its socket and catch him before he hit the ground.

Bernard gasped in horror.

The crowd on the ground gazed up and let out a collective scream.

Eugene flipped and was staring straight up into the air when he hit.

Thwap!

Eugene broke through a canvas awning.

Thwap!

And another . . .

He bounced off yet another, and rolled off the edge. . . .

Splash!

He finally hit, but it wasn't the pavement. He had fallen into a fountain.

For a moment he didn't move, and the crowd wondered if he were dead. But he was just in shock. He wasn't dead. Not now, possibly not for many years. He was very much alive!

In spite of his shock, he managed to sit up. He smiled, chuckled, and fell back into the water.

AFTER BEING CHECKED out at the hospital, Bernard and Eugene went back to Whit's End to relax.

Bernard was about ready to retire from janitorial work and run away to a Caribbean island. He was not one to enjoy excitement of any kind, and he had had enough excitement to last him a couple of lifetimes. He drank six glasses of water when he got to Whit's End.

But he was most of all happy to be alive. It didn't even occur to him until much later that he had just lost a major client when the Commerce Building went up in flames. It didn't faze him at all. It was just a building. Walton's Janitorial Service was just a business. All he was losing was money. It was all temporary—it would blow away in the wind. He would rather dwell on the things that were eternal.

Bernard was glad to find out that Eugene was not the madman who had blown up the Commerce Building. They were distant cousins, after all. In fact, no one had ever been prouder of Eugene. He had shown bravery, strength, and unselfishness in a very dangerous situation.

But as everyone gathered around to thank and congratulate their hero, Eugene was troubled. He had done things that day that he didn't realize he was capable of, both physically and emotionally. Why wasn't he *always* like that? Why did it take a face-to-face brush with death to bring out a sacrifice in him? Had he acted recklessly because he thought he was going to die anyway? Or had he acted sacrificially, putting others before himself, knowing that God's reward was coming in the end?

He contemplated the Bible verse in Philippians chapter 2 that says, "Do nothing out of selfish ambition or vain conceit, but in humility consider others better than yourselves."

Connie walked across the room in silence and brushed some soot from Eugene's vest.

"You lost a button. You need me to sew one on for you?"

"No thank you, Miss Kendall. I am well-versed in . . ." He stopped and watched her shake the soot from his pocket protector. Usually he would be annoyed by this. But now he realized that Connie was being like Jesus—a servant, thinking of others before she thought of herself.

"Actually, yes. I guess I would like some assistance."

Connie smiled. Eugene took off his vest and handed it to her.

Eugene decided then that he would treat every day as if it were his last. He would be more sensitive to other people. He would sacrifice his own needs for theirs. He would praise God for every day he had on earth.

And seeing an opportunity to thank God publicly, he would graciously accept "Eugene Meltsner Day."

The largest crowd in years gathered at the town center the next day. The mayor threw everything together in a matter of hours after she heard about Eugene's heroic deeds. Eugene stood proudly on the grandstand as a city councilman hung a medal around his neck.

"And so, for the uncommon bravery and selfless service he exhibited on behalf of this community, we award the Citizen's Medal of Valor to Eugene Felzner—"

"It's Meltsner," Eugene whispered.

"—as a small token of our gratitude."

Eugene smiled and looked out at all the fans. He didn't ever remember being in front of a crowd this large. A bead of sweat rolled down his forehead as he stood in front of the microphone.

"Greetings and—" Eugene was jarred by tremendous feedback from the microphone. The councilman stepped forward and motioned for him to step back a little. Eugene thanked him with a nod.

"Councilman Beasley . . . Mayor . . . friends and citizens of Odyssey . . . I thank you for this award. But it is *I* who am truly grateful. You see, if it were not for this experience, I'm afraid I never would have realized how truly blessed I am. I never would have realized how precious each moment—"

He stopped to swallow a lump in his throat. "Excuse me . . . I'm a little choked up, to borrow the colloquialism."

He regained his composure and cleared his throat. "Were it not for this experience, I never would have appreciated God's promise to me that my time here on earth, however brief, is not the end. I can now face my immortality without fear, knowing that I have a Savior, Jesus Christ, who will one day take me to be with him."

Eugene sniffed. "Some of you are probably aware that I lost my parents at a very young age. I have no brothers or sisters. . . . But Jesus is a friend who sticks closer than a brother. And I say to you that each of us has been blessed. In my case, I've been blessed with those people whom I know and love at Whit's End."

He looked out at his friends. Whit, Connie, Bernard, Dylan, and Jesse were all standing in the front row.

Connie wiped her eyes with her sleeve. Bernard took a step back, away from the others' view, and blew his nose loudly into a handkerchief.

Eugene's eyes were now filled with tears. He was glad he'd decided to memorize his speech instead of using note cards, because he wouldn't have been able to read them at this point.

He continued. "I simply want to encourage each of you to make the most of each precious moment you have with those you love. Because once it's gone, you'll never get the moment back."

Eugene bowed his head, and everyone thought he was done. There was scattered applause. But then Eugene poked his head back up and waved his hand to signal them to stop clapping for a moment. He pulled his ukulele from underneath the podium.

"To better illustrate this theme I have written a short lyrical melody that I would very much like to perform for you right now as a solo."

He began to strum and sing off-key.

"Oh, Eugene, don't wreck the moment with a song!" Bernard laughed.

He and the gang held their ears closed, while the rest of the crowd made a hasty exit. When Eugene looked up from his solo, he realized *he* was solo—except for his friends in the front row. "Uh . . . hello? Where did everybody go?"